AUTOBIOGRAPHY OF A CAT

Laura Novotny

Laura Violet Novotny

AUTOBIOGRAPHY OF A CAT

Written by Laura Violet Novotny

Cover Illustration by Stephanie Lake
Layout by Stacey Willey

Copyright © 2011 Laura Violet Novotny

Published by Natural Light Publishing
Gwinn Michigan 49841
www.myvioletbooks.com

Printing Coordinated by
Globe Printing, Ishpeming, Michigan
www.globeprinting.net

First Printing December 2011

ISBN 978-0-9848251-0-3

Printed in the United States of America

All Rights Reserved. No part of this document may be copied or reproduced in any way without the express written permission of the author.

Forward

    Few authors today have the gift or ability to capture the attention of both young and old, and to transport them to another world, yet, Laura Novotny has done just that. Her attention to detail and love of animals makes *Autobiography of a Cat* a book that transcends all ages. Instantly, the reader is engaged and enveloped within the world of the cat as the story captivates and carries the reader along an emotional journey filled with laughter and tears. The characters are familiar, warm and inviting as we share the journey with them.

    Laura writes with purity and an innocence that makes this story an appropriate wholesome family book 'purrfectly' poised to become a bedtime favorite for adult and child alike. So grab a blanket, turn off the television, and be prepared to get lost within the pages of a new modern-day classic.

– Cordelia D. Miller

Preface

I have always loved cats. I have owned so many, (or they have owned me), and have interacted with, and observed them, for so long, I feel as if I can see inside their minds. I thought about that one day, and wondered what a cat would say if it could tell about its life from a cat's point of view, re-living its own memories, from beginning to end. Loving to write as much as I love cats, I decided to take it on, and so emerged *Autobiography of a Cat*. It is a whimsical work, intended to entertain young and old alike. I have immensely enjoyed being the cat. However, I would interject that giving a cat the vocabulary liberties of a human was done only to add flavor to the story, as well as to offer a sense of understanding and compassion to the reader. A cat is just that. A cat. A cat is subject to humans, and limited in its understanding. A cat is a beautiful, mysterious, sensitive creature, created by God from His infinite imagination. I thank him for his grace, for his Son, for the gifts he has given – and for cats.

It has been a wonderful journey, being down there, peering out from a cat's eyes for a while. It's time for me to stand up now, and let you get down and have a look.

-- Laura Violet Novotny

Acknowledgements

To my husband, Steven.
Thank you, for the many hours of technical help, for encouraging me to keep writing, loving me and tolerating my cats.

To Cory.
You understand the power of the written word, and have kept me believing that someone will want to read mine.

To Mom and Dad.
I wish you were here, so I could sit in your kitchen and read my first book to you.

Introduction

This book is written for those who love and know cats well, or who would just like to learn about them, or simply be entertained by them. Though *Autobiography of a Cat* is written beyond the elementary reader level, it is perfect for reading to the very young, and an adventurous teaching tool for exposing them to many wonderful expressions of the English language.
--L.V.N.

LAURA VIOLET NOVOTNY

AUTOBIOGRAPHY OF A CAT

Two little girls are playing with kittens in the grass.
"I wish I had a million kittens!"
"Silly! How could you ever love a million kittens?"
"One at a time."

-Author Unknown

Chapter One

I remember being surrounded by warmth, with the sound of a beating heart and a rhythmic rumbling, which made me feel comfortable and safe. Suddenly, I felt a pressure which moved me forward through the darkness. I remember wetness, then I felt cold air, immediately followed by something rough but gentle and warm, massaging me quickly, and I became clean, and warm again. The familiar rumbling surrounded me again, but now, I heard a language I understood, uttered low; a smell and warm fuzziness I knew instinctively was my mother. I began to cry with want, as I moved toward my source of love. It seemed I was drawn to her soft belly, and when I found the warm teat, I latched on there eagerly, and so good and warm it was! I spread my arms in ecstasy and drank, and drank, and moved my paws against her mother-scented fur. I remember nothing but complete tranquility. Tiny purr...belly full...satisfied...sleep...sleep...

I rose to sleepy consciousness later, feeling other movement beside me. It remained dark, but I could tell I was not alone. There were others like me, also a source of warmth, to which I gravitated. The lovely nourishment kept us very sleepy, and eventually, we all piled against one another for a long doze, molded into a tight bundle. Milky breathing, warm fur, tiny hiccups, and the occasional twitches of digestion and growth, only seemed to lull us further into oblivion.

I awoke with a start. I keenly sniffed the air and sensed a new scent that was not my mother's. I spat and urgently sniffed into my dark world, not liking the new scent, or the feeling of empty space which surrounded me. My heart raced. Something warm enclosed me, and I was lifted up, up, up! I began to fling my feet frantically in all directions, all claws spread. I cried as loudly as I could, and immediately I heard the soothing trill of my mother's voice nearby. Whatever held me now, held me against more warmth, and I felt warm breath and a kiss gently placed on my head. Hearing the sound of my mother's distant purring below me, I began to relax a little at the cooing sounds this other nurturer made against my face. So there was more to my family than I thought. The extension of coddling eventually materialized itself into, first, this kindly person called Rachel, who, I found out later, lavished the same attention on my mother. I sensed my mother's relaxation whenever Rachel came into the room. I decided what was good for my mother, was certainly good enough to evoke purring from me. So, this I bestowed happily and often, especially when those kind hands would scratch me all over, and turn me on my back for the much-wanted attention to my belly. Oh, how I loved that! I seemed to have the best of worlds: Suckle, sleep, play, attention, all revolving in a continuous, serene existence. There were only a couple things against which I found I must rebel. One was the incessant attempts of my furry companions to steal away my suckling spots. We would constantly whine at one another, as we scratched at each other's heads angrily, pushing, shoving, stealing, always vying for position.

Another point of annoyance was being forced to lie still, as my mother gave me my frequent daily baths. No kitten was cleaner than I. When I tried to wriggle away, she would hold me firmly with her strong arm over my back. I would be tossed to and fro by her licking, eventually ending up on my back, as she cleaned my bottom – it seemed even that function was to be taken care of for me. However, all the jostling would inevitably end in the quiet peace of cuddling against her downy belly, as once again, I would eat until satisfied, my purring softer and softer, until it finally faded slowly into separate tiny dots, then stopped altogether.

Eventually, I found it more productive and enjoyable to incorporate play into these bathing encounters. I held my mother's face in my little paws, and bit with toothless gums wherever I felt her. She responded by uttering her soft maternal trills, and gentle pausing bites all over my body. She was great fun, and I, along with my companions, mourned her absence each time she left us to do whatever mothers go to do. As the days passed by, her absences grew longer, and we began to entertain ourselves in new ways, for, wonder of wonders, our space was not contained in this square enclosure in which we had been born. Curiosity got the best of us, as we began to move about, and when sight came with freedom, a whole new world of adventure opened up before us, as one day, sleep was not as important as finding the WAY OUT.

Chapter Two

The graceful leap which my mother used to exit our cardboard home was not so graceful an effort for me or my siblings. There were five of us in furry sum total, and I proudly admit that I was the first to attempt the 'leap fatale'. What my creator saved on me in fur to cover my slight form, he definitely doled out with abandon in curiosity and nerve. I took full advantage of both traits at every opportunity.

One opportunity was the top rim of this box, and I decided I was going to scale it –TODAY. I carefully toddled over to a wall chosen at random, sat down, looked straight up into space, got up, prepared to leap, sat back down again, then gave it everything my small body could muster, as I threw myself upward. I don't think I really expected to clear the 'wall into the unknown' on this first try. When I hit the wall with all twenty tiny claws flexed desperately, I found there was absolutely nothing to attach them to, and so, I slid back quickly, to plop backwards into a small heap onto the floor. I wriggled quickly to my feet, with a natural instinct welling up inside that I must never remain long in any clumsiness, and immediately attacked the wall again, this time with more fervor, and more determination. My leaping attempts became higher, my slides back down longer, and my backward tumbles more –tumbly. By this time, my partners in adventure had all joined me in full force, well, almost all. There was one sibling, my only brother, of medium size, (I was the smallest) who seemed to 'develop' a bit more slowly than the rest of us. He seemed content to sit in the opposite corner, playing among our 'swaddling clothes' the first day our break-out attempts began. He was quite entertained, as he tilted his little round face from side to side, ears perked, eyes big, watching our strange antics. His paw was outstretched, absentmindedly reaching here and there. We began to cry out, as we continued to jump, slide, tumble, jump, slide, tumble. Eventually, though, a couple of us managed to get a paw over the rim of our roofless room, for brief moments, only to fall from our own weight, back into our bed. Then, at last, after a brief, frustrated walk around our small perimeter, I stared at the wall one more time. I moved slowly up to it, positioned carefully, and gave it one more try. One paw over! Two paws over! I had a grip now, of the edge! I kicked and clawed furiously with both hind feet, mewing all the time at the effort, pointing my small nose upward, upward. I glimpsed the 'outside' for the first time! Space! Lots of it! I held myself there on the rim, peeking over. It was too overwhelming! I needed to get back down into the safety of our small room –but I could not. I was stuck there. I reached down sideways with my right paw, but my left claws just would not let go. In my excitement of first success, I had dug in deeply. My siblings, having had similar success, had all retreated safely back down, but here was I, hanging by one paw, with kicking feet, scratching frantically on the wall with all other three paws, not going forward, not going back. HELP! Mom! Help! Mom, apparently, was not within hearing distance of my kitten cries. Thank goodness, my other caregiver came quickly to my aid. She enclosed her hands gently around my taught little body, carefully unhooked the claws that were causing all the ruckus, and, after a much-needed cuddling and cooing in my ear, lowered me once more into my secure nest. If I HAD left, I would never have been so happy to be back home.

We all clamored for more attention, and the ensuing playtime with Rachel made us all forget our doleful attempt, and soon we were huddling for a nap. Quiet reigned once again in our humble space, and we were all unconscious for quite some time, in various and sundry positions and locations, among the soft kitten-scented folds.

Chapter Three

Well, I'd done it now. I had braved the escape over the wall, and here I was, upside-down, one back foot claw-hooked desperately on the top rim of the cardboard again, and all other paws spread wide with absolutely no traction, as I was sliding straight down! No turning back this time! I was first, as usual. I finally let go, and my slight weight landed me with a slight thud. I stood still for a few seconds, sniffing the air, checking my location with a delicious mixture of fear and curiosity. The curiosity part caused my feet to move cautiously forward, as I was vaguely aware of the commotion behind me. My bravery became contagious, as, one by one, each of my siblings did the same no-turning-back-now inverted scratch slide down the outside of our cardboard home. There were a few plaintive meows coming from inside the box, as my slower brother found himself alone for the first time. However, he, too, found his way out eventually, to join our new adventure.

The rest of us were like a little team of cloned robots at first –all poised the same: Tails straight out behind us, bodies stiff, carefully putting one paw in front of the other, sniffing intensely. We eventually relaxed our step, as we moved out in different directions. We met up with one foreign object after another, each getting its proper sniffing inspection. Sometimes, we would bump our noses when we sniffed out a new shape, jerking back our heads, or a paw, when we –heaven, forbid!– TOUCHED something. Every nerve in our little furry bodies was tuned on highest frequency. We were focused, alert little exploring creatures, about to invade our caregiver's home. Nothing would stop us now. The home box was old, tired territory. We had expanded our horizons. We were FREE, and none of us had any idea of the fun, the adventures – and the temptations – that awaited us in this new frontier.

Chapter Four

All eyes were on our little box room. Rachel had come in while we were again at our, now routine, big room play. She was kneeling down in front of the box, using some kind of tool to cut into it! We all lined up and sat in a little row, all ears identically forward, all heads tilting first to one side, then the other, all eyes wide with wonder, watching her movements. She introduced each of us, in turn, to the new entrance into our little box nest. I stopped, as we all did, – well, all except our brother – to sniff every inch of this new little opening, rubbing my mouth along its edge, marking it as my property. In and out of it we came, fascinated, as usual, by the smallest new things. Now, this was progress! Scaling the wall had been perfected, yes, but still quite a feat to perform. However, this! This was as it should be. Eat, nap, wake up, and simply walk (or leap!) out the door to go play! Run back through the door, eat, sleep, and play some more.

The time came, though, when we outgrew the box completely. Our mother nursed us on the floor then, wherever she decided to lie down. We would all come scrambling for our easy meal. Also, Rachel had introduced us to the 'litter box'. This had proved to be a wonderful source of entertainment, as well as a place where our 'task and bury' instincts could be fulfilled. Plowing through the gravelly stuff with our paws outspread and scattering it in all directions, was too much fun! Rachel often scolded us for the stuff that escaped the litter box perimeters, but we did it anyway, as kittens will do, forgetting the rules until the next scolding. The litter box plowing game was surpassed only by our discovery, one day, of the TOP OF THE BED. It seems we had been installed in a spare bedroom, and the day I learned to keep climbing up the bed leg, and catching hold of the bedspread, was a day of great vertical discovery. The others followed me, one by one, as we did everything, it seemed, in gradual unison, you might say – one following another into the next conquest. I got to the top first, grabbed on, dangled occasionally, and eventually came over the soft, fluffy horizon. My three sisters followed, and there we were again, doing the careful walk-and-sniff routine, all of us lined up, moving forward like an advancing front line, as our brother sat flat-butt still, down on the floor, looking up at us in wonder. He made his way up eventually, in his own way and in his own time.

 Run! Jump! Tackle! TRACTION! We had discovered a virtual padded playing field! It was so soft and wonderful on our little feet! The bed had officially become our favorite playground. Oh, the CLIMB! Falling down off it became as entertaining as tearing our way back up to the top. Rachel apparently thought so, too, for she often sat on the floor to watch us, and our antics caused her to throw her head back in laughter. We loved having her there, and she interacted with us a lot. We chased her hands endlessly, and sometimes we caught them, throwing ourselves on our sides, all fours holding on, kicking, biting, purring all the while. When Rachel threw a rolling toy, we all dashed after it as a group, jumping over one another as we went for the pounce. She was easily as much fun as our mother. We especially liked the fact that Rachel did not bite back like mama did. She didn't have claws, either, but then, our mother did not have the ability to scoop us into sudden air-born displacement when we climbed onto something off limits, or a spot which, after our arrival, proved to strand us helplessly. The bedroom curtains were one such vertical temptation, which proved to be both off limits and a place to get stranded. My first curtain nab left my feet dangling in mid air. I had climbed in frantic play up onto a chair. My gaze went higher to something hanging above me, against a huge wall. Another bed? One way to find out! I positioned my feet carefully, hunched down, padded my feet several times, then jumped. I grabbed on to the material with my front claws and immediately decided that down was a better direction, but 'down' was very far away! I held on, desperately crying and kicking my feet. There was nowhere to go but up! So up I went, clawing, climbing, crying, clawing, climbing. Hands suddenly grabbed me, trying to pry me loose.

"No, no! Not the curtain! Bad kitty!" Rachel scolded.

Well, the scolding only added to my fright at being pried off the only thing that kept me from falling into the abyss! As soon as she disengaged both front paws, I had already dug another front claw securely in again. On we went, me screaming, her scolding, hind feet finally out, front claws dug back in and climbing! I was finally parted from the curtains with no small effort on Rachel's part. I had left my mark. It was not the last time I found myself up there, and we each had our turn. So more curtain extractions occurred throughout the next few days, as our little army continued our upward attacks. The curtains soon displayed many scars of our endeavors. We learned to read our level of offense by the tone of even Rachel's walk, as she came to referee our latest mischief. We would then scatter and hide, if we were not attached to something.

More often than not, though, she came to play with us, and one day, she had a new lilt in her voice. She came carrying something new into the room. We all came running with tails up, meowing our curiosity. What new adventure now?

"Ok, everybody! Today, we learn to EAT!" she said.

Chapter Five

A shallow round object sat on the floor in front of us. We all surrounded it slowly, heads down, sniffing this new aroma which came from it. It smelled good. I approached the rim with trepidation, and did the usual sniff-jerk. Gradually, I sniffed further down into the object, and suddenly my nose dipped into something warm and wet. I sneezed and shook my head and sniffed some more. My nose got wet again, and again I sneezed, and licked it off. It was a strange taste, but not a bad taste, but it wasn't mom. I turned and walked away. My siblings did the same, in turn, except, of course, my brother. He never even went over to the spot. He simply watched us a minute, head tilted to one side slightly, and went to chase the ball that jingled.

The next experience was not at all pleasant. Apparently, learning to eat solid food was not an option. It was a forced necessity. I would have been perfectly happy to nestle and suckle at my mother's belly forever, but she had been discouraging us of that lately. It was a shock of rejection that we had never felt before. It was gradual, but it was there. So this strange new substance must be the second part of that plan. It was the WEANING EXPERIENCE. An unpleasant part of every kitten's life, and, now, even Rachel was turning on us. In no uncertain terms, she gently opened our mouths, one by one, and introduced a soft, wet food into them. At first, we fought against this indignity with vigor. However, when we got a good taste of the stuff, and began actually chewing, we forgot our objections, and wanted more. We finally got the hang of retrieving the solid food, be it by paw, or by mouth, from what Rachel called the 'dish'. It was a slow process; we were clumsy, messy and sneezed on each other. We walked in it and ran through it. When we really got into it, we overstuffed ourselves. This new way of eating was really satisfying, and it turned out that our brother, who always brought up the rear, became the first at the food dish. He sometimes regurgitated from gorging himself. He learned to moderate his eating, though, and soon was eating more slowly, which was much more in tune with everything else he did. As we all grew from our new nourishment, he grew past us in size, and was by far the largest now. I continued to come in last in the size category. My vim, vigor, leaping abilities, and courage, however, more than compensated for my small stature. One day, the big door was left open, and I lost no time in being the first one to go through it.

Chapter Six

There were two vistas that made up our new world of exploration in the room beyond the bedroom. The horizontal was straight ahead, around, and under. The vertical, well, the vertical got us into all kinds of trouble. It involved – no, required – a lot of climbing, in order to get from our point A, to our desired point B. Unfortunately, we were to discover that point B was not always a convenient place to be. However, horizontal was first. We began a more relaxed walk-and-sniff posture, as we made our way around this 'room that held our room'. It was quiet for now, but our sound sensors were still alert, as we moved silently about the new uncharted territory. We encountered many vertical pole-like objects, and sneaked around many corners. We stayed close against these 'walls', as they made us feel secure to be near something that offered hiding. Whenever we ventured into the open space of the room, we would instinctively feel more vulnerable, crying with uncertainty, until we would run to the nearest object, again calm and in exploring mode.

I was making my way along one of those large walls and happened to turn the corner at exactly the same time my 'slow brother' did. We bumped noses and simultaneously went up on our hind feet in terrifying surprise. I did a crooked backward leap, then landed my front feet facing my threat, heart pounding, ears twitching, fur puffed up. My brother, on the other hand, had simply jerked back his head once, upon our surprise encounter, and had stood, ears forward, calmly watching my over-reactive display. His tail was up, familiar front paw poised in mid-air. I twitched my tail and arched my back. We both found this quite amusing at the same moment, and began our side-way prancing and short forward jumps which always preceded play. The attack and tumbles followed, and soon the others joined in. Our serious exploring was temporarily postponed by this delightful distraction. The 'poles', we soon realized, were attached to chairs, tables and other assorted objects which promised enticing vertical temptations. They served as wonderful playtime things. We perfected the surprise meetings at the corners. We watched for them, hoped for them! These sudden surprise encounters drove us into wild fits of frenzied play. I rounded one corner at a run, and met one of my sisters there. She was also on a run, and when our noses bunted, we both leaped straight up into the air as if there were little springs on our feet, and I vow, we turned around in mid air, for we were heading in different directions when we hit the ground running! We raced to and fro in our wild freedom and abandon, climbing up chair legs and leaping down on our next victim. Tumbling, biting, clawing, running in cowardly terror, then prancing sideways back again, ears pinned back, once again General in Command. Oh, we had fun that first day in this new room! Our joy trilled up from our throats as we romped. We relished our careless, innocent life as kittens. We could not imagine there could be anything more interesting than this new outside world! Then we heard Rachel's familiar footsteps, as she approached. We saw another big door open as she entered the room. That great, tall door moving inward frightened us all out of our antics, and we scattered like roaches when the light comes on. We chose the nearest pre-discovered hiding places, and just the tips of five little faces peeked out at the sound of Rachel's voice.

"So, what's this? You finally found your way out, did you? Well, I just bet I know who instigated that!" she said.

She made her way straight to me, the accused. Oh, she knew us well, and we knew her, too. I did not run when she reached down to scoop me up. I purred contentedly against her cheek, as she cooed to me and praised me for my accomplishments. It was good to be held and coddled after my high-stress morning. I guess the others felt the same, for, one by one, they came out from their places of hiding, purring and begging Rachel's attention. She plopped herself down on the floor right where she stood, and gathered us all onto her lap. What a nice place that was to be! Warm and enveloping, two things we loved. She talked to us, and we trilled and purred until we were quite overcome by the need to sleep. It was about that time that our mother went into the bedroom, tail straight up, calling to us and, finding the room empty, demanded with loud yowls, that we all return immediately. I, for one, had no idea how we would accomplish that, since it had taken us three whole days to get OUT of there. We were not to worry. Rachel gently placed us, one by one, against our mama's belly, which was already bared invitingly for our mid-morning snack. Our food dish was good, but this was always better. We suckled, kneaded, and purred, then became silent. We drifted off into kitten dreams of great high walls and furniture legs and going back home, our mother warm and licking us all over. (That part may have been real.) I could not believe my world could get any better – but it did.

Chapter Seven

Would the wonders never end? We were absolutely amazed to find yet another, much larger world outside this one which we had recently discovered. We filed out through the big door, with me leading the march, as usual. We were all a little bolder now, having gotten good at this exploration thing. Even our larger but slower brother was bringing up the rear quite admirably. There were many more things out here that had those delightful pole legs we all so enjoyed. Oh, and the walls and corners here seemed to go on forever! There were objects of every description throughout this next new territory. We began to search and inspect it, room by room. So this was the rest of what we learned was the 'house' ! Our work was now endless! There was so much to do, so many places to get into, under, or on top of, and we learned them all. We frequented those that were most entertaining, one of which was upholstered furniture. It gave us the most 'tread' – even our slower brother could keep up, on that! Carpet was great fun, too. We became quite adept at sharpening our claws on both, though that often earned us a sharp reprimand from Rachel. We learned in 'trial by exploration' what was fun, what was hot, what was wet, what was deep, what moved easily, where to hide, where NOT to hide, what to climb, and what to climb when Rachel was gone. In other words, what got reprimands, and what did not! The strangest and most curious item we discovered, was located in the big 'living room'. It was brought to our attention when it gave off a loud, shrill, singing noise, which drew us all to it irresistibly. Sometimes, it would make a strange click, and we would hear Rachel's voice inside the box it sat on. We would all run to the sound of her voice, but she would not be there. We would meow, and walk around it, pawing at it, trying to find her. Then other strange voices would come out of it and it would click again and eventually go silent. We learned to walk on top of its little buttons and cause other strange things to happen. When Rachel was at home, we learned that she would always go to the strange thing when it sang, and so we would run to it when we heard it, for that reason alone. We would then pile on her, if she sat with the thing to talk. We crawled all over her shoulders and neck, with mass, earnest purring. We were happy just to hear the drone of her familiar voice. She absentmindedly scratched and tickled us all in turn, as we vied for position up against her face and throat. When we all became overly enthusiastic, she would begin to pluck us off, one after the other, like so many little burs on her clothes. It was a comical rotation of 'crawl back to neck, get plucked off and put back in lap, then crawl back to neck again'. This plucking us off, too, was done absentmindedly, as she talked to the object in her hand. By the end of her visit with this object, which we learned to be the 'telephone', she would have plucked off a sum total of about thirty of us little burs. The telephone, then, became our 'dinner bell' for time with Rachel – something we ate up delightedly at every opportunity. When the phone calls were over, we would all eventually be extracted from her torso and she would walk away to her own concerns. We would easily return to our frolic and fun all over the house. We would sometimes be joined by our mother. She became a kitten herself, when she played and romped with us. She seemed to enjoy it as much as we did. She always won the play wrestles, of course, but she was gentle and loving with us, most of the time. We would get our bite or spit of discipline when we needed it. She was a playmate to us, but we respected her authority. We did not realize at the time, that all the play actually were lessons of offense and defense for our lives as adults. Hunting skills and fighting skills were all intertwined in our playtime. It was all part of the wondrous instincts given to our mother by the Creator, and passed on to us, so we could do the same some day, with our offspring. We were all part of God's universal plan for things. Some things, however, were only learned by trial and error. There were plenty of those lessons yet in front of us. Many of them were learned in what we found to be the most entertaining room in the house. I will never forget the day we discovered THE KITCHEN.

Chapter Eight

As much fun as it was to go snagging across a carpeted, upholstered room, there was a certain joyful abandon in running at top speed, in a high speed chase, onto the tiled kitchen floor. We would slide into an attempt to stop, sometimes slamming on our sides, as all four feet kept going. Feet still in running mode, we would pop back up, running in place, only to spring straight up, to avoid an incoming kitten. We would often meet each other in the air, and land, still running, as we tore back out of the kitchen. The slippery floors weren't the only joys of this special room. It was the place where family often mingled. It was the place that was so warm when Rachel cooked. It was the place with the FOOD. Dining properly when we were called, was nice. Stalking through the kitchen when no persons were there, especially at night, now that was the real adventure! We would sometimes climb to heights unknown, to search out the source of some delectable scent. No exposed crumb or morsel was safe from our sampling. Our greatest fear was sudden lights on and Rachel scattering us in all directions.

My first kitchen adventure, when I was much younger and less wise, was quite an ordeal for all involved. Of the five of us, I was the first, of course, to make my way up to the top of the 'great mountain' – the kitchen table. The others were testing some other unknown objects, and there was our slow brother, sitting in the corner, completely satisfied to bat around a dry, dead fly the whole time. I sniffed my way to a tall shiny object that had been left on the table, from the dinner gathering. It had a familiar scent I was quite partial to at that age – MILK! I walked slowly across the table surface, and gently, carefully, stood up on my hind legs to place my paws, one at a time, on the object's cold surface. I pulled one paw back quickly at the first contact, but my bravery took over, and I began to reach for the top edge –there had to be a way to get – SWOOSH! Back I went, as a huge splash of white washed over me! The object fell over noisily, rolled, and crashed onto the floor below. Frightened and drenched, I scurried and slid, and fell on my back. I scrambled quickly to my feet to escape the attacking milk. As I exited the slippery, white-pooled mountain top, air-born, Rachel came running in at the sound of the commotion. My siblings had all scrambled with surprise as well, knocking over other kitchen objects. I was already on the ground and running, shaking off milk in fits and starts. I finally stopped, deciding cleanliness was my first priority for the moment. Rachel never frightened me too much, and so I licked my fur frantically, getting the taste of milk with every effort. I never enjoyed my bath so much! My siblings came tiptoeing up to investigate, and to lick some of their own dots of milk which landed on them as I repeatedly shook my fur. Rachel continued to click and sputter her mild disapproval at what I had done. We all got a general lecture, but there was as much purring going on as regretting. It was just one of our many learning experiences. I learned at least two important things: Do not attempt to drink from any container of milk taller than you are, and don't let anyone share your bath when it tastes so good!

Chapter Nine

Since our new independence, our natural mother had become more of a friend and playmate to us now. She walked among us occasionally, but we were a preoccupied and involved bunch. We still enjoyed playing around her, and were now actually quite good at our ambush tactics. She would play along patiently until our rambunctious antics got past her patience. Then, we would learn her bite-and-hold lessons of combat. Some of these lessons would actually make us cry out in pain. However, these painful lessons were always immediately followed by profuse licking and purring, both to show her good intentions, and often just to clean up the spots we missed. Eventually, we saw less and less of her. It seemed natural, and acceptable. We lived our parallel lives in a cat's contentment.

~~~

There were several things that we learned were constants in our new environment. Lampshades LOOK stationary, but once jumped onto, never are. Vases, no matter what shape or size, are NEVER a good thing to tip over; they earned us sharp reprimands from Rachel, whether she was present during the incident, or not. If the tipped vase was filled with water and flowers? Hide for a minimum of one hour. If stepping into something brown, sticky, or wet, find a hidden spot to immediately begin paw grooming. It is just too difficult to do while being frantically chased by Rachel. Chewing on plants and digging in their soil could earn you a line-up and paw inspection that was terrifying. The clean-up was not pleasant, and soil was only second to sticky, in wipe-off indignity. Of course, Rachel lectured us during the whole process. There I would be, hanging helplessly in one of her hands, while she rubbed or wiped my feet and tail with the other hand, all the while voicing her disapproval. There was nothing to do but pin back my ears, cry pitifully, hold on for dear life, plead for it all to end soon, and run to the nearest hiding place, as soon as my clean feet hit the floor. After a few prideful licks to my horribly disturbed fur, and a couple complete body shakes, I usually made my way, carefully, back to the plant that had caused all the trouble, got the last sniff and sneer, then, remembering, leaped away to alternate entertainment.

Lastly, and most important, we learned that napping for long periods of time, and as often as possible, is the most assured way of staying out of trouble.

So, the days flew by, and we learned many more things, some useful, most not. The mysterious 'door to the outside', located in the kitchen, was a constant curiosity to us. Often, when it would open and close, we rushed up to breathe the wonderful draft that came from 'outside', whatever that was. Outside was still a mystery to us, and we knew the wonders of discovery did not stop at our present environment. We were desperately guarded away from going through that door. The foot swipes, pushing us away when we tried, eventually discouraged our attempts to dash out the door. Rachel would only say 'You have to stay inside, you're too little, and there are too many things to hurt you out there'. Well, I seemed to remember 'many things' that had hurt us in HERE, and the fun was always worth it. So, 'outside' must be the adventure of all adventures! I, for one, made it my private goal in life to make it through that door. I did make it through one day, but in a way I had never imagined.

Chapter Ten

It was always an amusing time when visitors came in. Even during our most involved and focused play, our ears were acutely attuned to the sound of the kitchen door opening or closing. Most of the time, it was one of our own household members coming or going, which almost always evoked a group greeting. However, occasionally, a strange and new scent would float through the house, and going to investigate was irresistible. We would advance in stealth, troop of five, around corners, under chairs, skittering down the side of the hallway, until we reached the opening into the kitchen. We would peek in from different vantage points, eyes wide, ears up, tails down, noses working overtime, waiting to be beckoned. We usually always were called to the visitors, who would often administer over-enthusiastic ravaging. This we endured with tails up, and the utmost purring and conversational meowing. It was always an occasion for much affection, even though some of the smaller visitors were not adept at the proper handling of a real living, breathing, furry kitten. Some of them would act as if we were one of those musty, still, lifeless creatures that slept constantly, and collected dust. These small visitors were noisy and not careful about where they walked, and we got quite good at knowing which visitors to avoid. There was only one plan of action for those kind: Run the other way to the nearest, most distant hiding place!

One morning, in the middle of romp-and-tear time, the mysterious door to the outside opened, and some people came in and were led directly to us. This was not a common procedure. Visitors usually stopped directly in the kitchen or dining area, and visited there with Rachel. We were usually only a short source of show-and-tell, later in the hour, or sooner, if one or more of us ambled in to snoop. Usually, we would greet a visitor, or group of visitors, every few days. Some were quite familiar to us. However, today, they were unfamiliar and they came one after another. The visitors sought US out. Rachel was telling them all about each of us, as the visitors, in turn, picked up each of us, cooed, smiled, petted, tickled and generally bombarded Rachel with questions of our care. I heard the sound of insecure crying, as one of my siblings was carried away, out of the room. Rachel walked with them, and I heard the door close and the talking stop. So did the cries of my sibling. We never saw her again. She was nowhere in the house. We looked everywhere. We called to her, as we often did when we became separated in our great domain. It became clear, over the next few days, that visitors meant the continuing depletion of our little group. There came the day when only my slower-than-normal brother, and I, were left. The cries of my absent siblings still haunted me and made me nervous. My more mild sibling seemed not to care much, and took in everything with patient observance. My plan was much different. I had quite enough of frightful scoop-ups and disappearing acts. Now, when a strange scent was in the draft, I ran, and I ran hard. I pinned my ears back for least resistance and utilized my most effective hiding places. I feared terribly having the same unknown end as my predecessors.

Alas, it was a futile effort. Rachel sought me out, with every convincing effort, and ultimately had to drag me, all twenty claws desperately dug in, from underneath my not-so-secure armchair bunker. My claws popped on the carpet all the way, until they were disconnected from the fibers individually. I was handed, fighting, to the stranger. My heart was beating terribly, so that my little chest might burst. I pinned my ears to show I was serious, and cried out for dear life. My captor had a co-conspirator, whose strange scent filled my senses and only made me more terrified. The one who held me immediately sounded apologetic, cooing and awing in my ear, as she nestled me against her, just under her chin. She wrapped me gently but firmly in her hands to calm my squirms and hysteria. She breathed into my fur, and continued to console me. Her voice was high, and soothing. When she began to massage my neck in little circles, I began to slowly relax, and so did my heartbeat and cries. I began to whimper helplessly, with half-cries. She seemed to 'hear' me saying, 'Who are you? What is about to happen to me?' I felt the vibration of this stranger's voice against me, as she spoke.

There was a different note in Rachel's voice. It was weaker somehow, and, yes, it was quivering. I sensed a sadness as she reached to touch me in my stranger's arms, and suddenly, she stepped up and kissed me quickly on the top of my head. I was buried in these new arms, and I felt us move toward the kitchen door. So, this was it. This was my own disappearing act. Now I would know what had happened to the others. As I was carried away, I looked back once to see my little brother peeking into the kitchen. He didn't look frightened, only excitedly interested. I hoped he would be alright. Somehow, I knew he would be.

As we went out into the fresh air, I was given no time to examine the outdoors that I had waited so long to see. I had a fleeting sense of wondering how I would find my way back to Rachel. Then, I heard her familiar voice, the one I had known since birth, call goodbye to us, and then it was gone.

I had settled down in these new arms to some extent, until I was taken into the little loud room that moved. I had heard its rumble before, but at a distance. What I soon learned to be 'the car', was simply another word for a terrifying experience! First, the slamming of the doors caused a definite change in pressure, to which I was acutely sensible. Then, the noise of this obnoxious room was enough to send any abducted kitten into a frenzy. I clawed out of my temporary warm refuge, and had escaped too quickly for her to catch me. I grabbed the first thing claws could sink into, and kept on scrambling until I was over the seat and under it in less time than it takes to say 'run'! My soothing companion eventually extracted me from under the car seat, but not without my less-than-eloquent protests. Once she had me firmly imbedded inside her sweater, her driver, and co-conspirator in this ruining of a perfectly good morning, took us toward the next Great Unknown in my life.

~~~

When we finally escaped the moving noisy terror, I was carried into a house. I was briefly introduced to the man who had driven the get-away car. His was a much less affectionate greeting. It consisted of a couple short pats on my head and a half-scratch on my neck. I was let down to the floor, supposedly to explore my new environs at leisure. I hit that floor running and advanced forthwith to the first available place to take cover. I heard the man and woman talk about letting me go, to get to know the place and that I'd be alright. Well, why wasn't I convinced of that? I sat fearfully still for quite some time, aware of every movement and scent and sound. My nerves had been in so much overdrive, I began to relax, in spite of myself, from sheer fatigue. I moved quietly from underneath one structure to another. I moved from this room, to the next. It also had the soft carpeting, which was foreign, but comforted me somehow. This was all accompanied by coos and sweet words from my new companion, who seemed to be trying desperately to calm me from a distance. I could see her peeking at me from where I hunkered under the couch that I had finally settled on for my barricade. Her words and soothing speech did help, and soon it grew quiet, and a kitten's need for sleep, made me feel drowsy. I purred a little when she very slowly reached under the couch to scratch my neck. She left me alone then, and, somehow knowing any immediate threat or danger had passed, I fell slowly asleep. Not the comforting, rolled-in-a-ball kind of nap I was used to, but hunched upright, on all fours, tail tucked tightly from insecurity, and eyes closing sleepily, because fright is a very tiresome thing.

Chapter Eleven

I awoke, curled on my side, and to the sound of Sara's voice. That was her name. She kept saying it.

"Come to Sara! Come to mommy. I have something yummy for you!" she coaxed.

She was showing me a small bowl, from which was inundating a delightful odor. I hadn't realized my hunger through all the unpleasant excitement, and now my survival instincts, and Sara's cooing words, beckoned me from my hiding place. I crawled out slowly, meowing hesitantly, sniffing the good scent of nourishment. I began lapping at the delicious warm milk. How good it tasted! There was a sweet comfort to this moment –here, close to Sara, accepting her sweet offering. Fleeting thoughts of my own mother's warm, comforting fur, and her soothing sounds and milky smells, somehow fused and intermingled, so that I began to trust this new person, who obviously was trying to show her love to me. Those thoughts consumed me now, so that when she reached out to touch me with a single finger running gently down my back, I responded by lifting my tail and looking up at her. Suddenly, purring escaped from me, profuse purring, desperate purring. I was saying, 'Yes! Please love me! Please hold me and comfort me! I don't understand what has happened to me, and I don't know where I am, or where my mother is, or where Rachel is! I am scared, and I need to trust someone'. She scooped me up then, and this time I didn't fight. I gave in to the affections she offered to me, and I returned them. I stayed close to her for the next few days, until I got braver and more secure. I often slept in her cozy lap, and we both got to know each other. It didn't take me long to know that this was my new 'mother', and that the man in the house was someone who loved her, too, but who didn't love me. For now, it was alright. My lively spirit soon revived, and I was ready for my next adventure. It was time to get to know my new home.

My new surroundings were different, but contained most of the same series of wooden legs, doorways, and hallways around which to maneuver. My confusion of sudden displacement was soon overshadowed by my relentless need to explore every new inch, and this I did, with a little fear and trepidation. At first, I moved from underneath one object to the next, never letting myself remain in the vulnerability of wide open space. However, I began having lapses of play, when I would spy something of interest that moved, or didn't move, and I would then pounce out at it from my protective lair. I would suddenly realize I was exposed in another strange location, only to dart back under the nearest cover. This sequence of lapse and dart, lapse and dart, continued until I had pretty much discovered every crevice I could fit into, or through. Actually, this took a period of several days, but it kept me busy and there were plenty of daily snuggles and coos from Sara. So, my earlier life eventually faded into distant memories, and I began to settle into my new domain. It would be Sara and James from now on. Heaven forbid that I would ever be abducted again! So, I was loved again, by one, and tolerated by the other. It was a bit more of a challenge getting to know James, but I made every attempt, though he did not, on his part, make any attempt to get to know me. Being the active and spirited cat I was, I rather enjoyed my adventures with James. It was a game with me, all the more enjoyable because I knew it was not a game with him. A lover of cats he was not, that was clear, but my new friend and protector, Sara, gave me daily assurance that I was in no danger. I was cared for like never before, and I had a home again, with one very agreeable difference: It was all mine! All Sara's attention was for ME. I did not have to share it with any other cats. That was something I got used to, in no time at all. It was a role I assumed quite well.

～～～

It was not long before I became quite familiar with Sara's routine. I was aware of her at all times, whether she realized it or not. I was always close at hand when her 'quiet time' came each morning. It was always just Sara and me. Always the same time, the same cozy chair, and the same book. Sara called it the Bible, God's word. She explained all about what that meant when I was a kitten, playing and moving about on her lap. I listened while I pounced at everything that moved or dotted, or dangled. The ribbon that held her place in the Bible would forever have my mark, as I repeatedly attacked its irresistible movement with claws and teeth. My more half-hearted attacks on that ribbon would continue into my adulthood, while I purred, just happy to spend the time with Sara. It was our own little quiet time game, and neither of us minded at all. In all the years from a kitten to a full-grown cat, this was my favorite time of day, and I think it was hers, too. She knew very well that, as soon as she sat down, I would jump up and walk directly onto the open book, and lie down with great ease upon its pages. She would slide me aside with smiling ceremony, as I stayed in position, purring all the while. As I approached sleep, I would stretch my arms out full length across the chapters, and again, she would simply lay them aside, as she continued to read. Sometimes, she would read the scriptures aloud, and I would look into her eyes, as she told me how I was created out of God's wonderful imagination. I would begin to blink with sleepiness, lulled by sheer contentment at the sound of her voice, sensing something that was innate in me, about my Creator. My purrs were deep and loud. By the time she prayed, I was usually approaching motionless slumber, with the gentle weight of her hand on my fur.

Chapter Twelve

There was a new excitement throughout the house. The conversation between Sara and James was animated. They smiled and laughed, and talked of the 'new addition'. Well, I could only speculate what that could be, but eventually, I gathered that my human family was going to expand, as over time, Sara's tummy did. After several months, my private lap space was severely compromised. I managed to find some room there anyway, and Sara laughed at my squirming and repositioning during my cuddle moments with her. Sometimes, I would just give up and crawl carefully over the big mound of her belly, and stretch out with my paws on her shoulders. Sometimes, I felt a strange movement under me, and my puzzled appearance made Sara giggle. I would stare at her with my sleepy eyes, and she would smile dreamily with love in her own eyes. I was suspicious that her smile was not just for me, as she hummed a lullaby, and stroked my head and back. They were happy days, expectant days, days of waiting. As the time drew near for this big event, I went about my daily routine, wondering how my life might change. I never felt slighted for affection, though. No matter how much Sara was preoccupied with the coming event, she always found time for me. I was always welcome, and even involved, in special moments of nursery inspection. I batted the dangling toys, did carefully-balanced catwalks on the delicate furniture, chased and tangled ribbons. This new little person could mean lots of entertainment for me, and Sara and I 'talked' of it a great deal. Well –she talked, and I obediently listened, purred, and chirped my encouragement.

~~~

One day, I silently entered an unusually quiet living room, where Sara sat alone, as John was away at work. She stared straight ahead, not smiling, with both hands on her belly, and I, sensing something was wrong, quietly came to her and jumped up onto the arm of her chair. I rested one front paw on her arm, and reached up to touch her cheek with my nose. She seemed to come to herself and reached out a hand to pet me, without speaking. That was odd.

Later, after John came home, they spoke quietly, he hugged her, and, after a phone call was made, they both left the house. I was uncomfortable and nervous, without knowing why. I lay down in her chair and dozed uneasily, listening intently for their return.

~~~

I did not see Sara again for several days. James came in and out, to feed me, and take care of things. I watched and waited.

When James finally brought Sara back, she stayed in bed for some time. I stayed near her whenever I could, during the day, and sometimes slipped onto the bed in the darkness, to sleep against her. I could tell she was glad to have my company. When she eventually sat in her chair, I eased into her lap, which no longer lacked for room, and offered my soft fur, my calming purr, my quiet presence. I was something warm to hold when she cried. Whatever events happened in the next few days, we all experienced them together, from the viewpoints of both the grieving human heart, and the watchful eye of a faithful cat, who kept a vigil day and night.

    I sat quietly and watched at a distance, in an understood reverence, when John and Sara held each other and prayed. They did that often anyway, holding hands at their study time, when they read the Bible together. They always prayed at the kitchen table, but recently those prayers were desperate and seeking. In those moments, as they made their plea for 'grace and strength', there was something in the room that could be felt. There was another Presence here, I knew it. I knew it deep inside me. It was a presence of something or someone strong, and caring, and good. It was something I knew I was part of –my 'creator', as Sara had said. She thanked God for me sometimes. I never knew he had any part of bringing me here, but if Sara said he did, then it was probably true, and certainly more than a cat could understand.

Chapter Thirteen

I had never before seen Sara dressed completely in black. I didn't like it, because I also had never seen her so sad. James and Sara left for the afternoon like that, and, fatigued from worry, I slept. When they returned, we three spent a long quiet evening, with no one talking much at all. I simply walked slowly and meaninglessly from room to room, sitting at intervals. I noticed Sara did the same thing. James eventually disappeared off by himself somewhere in the house. I didn't understand much of exactly what had happened, but I knew that for now, it would be just the three of us for a while longer.

The melancholy quietness continued to lay on the household. In the days that followed, I felt it keenly in all of my senses, making me unusually sensitive to every mood and movement of my human family. Sara would always scoop me up in those moments when she needed the softness of my fur and the warmth of my purring to comfort her. I gladly yielded, as always, for I had as much to gain, in feeling her need of me. I knew I was always welcome when I slipped up onto her lap, at those times when I sensed her in sad repose. There was no hesitation, not ever, with her.

Today, when I walked into the big room where James' old easy chair was, anyone would have thought, from the silence, that he was not there. I knew he was. I sensed him, before I saw him. Normally, unlike Sara, he was never eager to show me much affection, or welcome mine. Normally, I would have chosen a different room now, for my meandering. I would have waited until the big chair was empty, to safely steal a nap there. I would do so, even at the risk of being unmercifully banished, by James, from a perfectly good sleep.

"Get down, cat!" he would say impatiently, "You think this is YOUR chair?"

I seldom was caught in the act of stealing his chair, but when I was, the insult was always worse than the injury, which was only to my dignity. The message I got from James was clearly understood. I accepted it, and slept in the big chair only by stealth. I certainly would exit as quietly, and as quickly, as I would sense his presence.

So, the thing that moved me forward now into the room, was not coming from the calm assurance that he was not there, but that he was. I chose my trail through the room easily, led completely by the highly-tuned senses that propelled me on, strangely unaware of any other instinct, but that I must go to him. I had gone to the lap, many times, of another, whom he loved as I did, and I knew what to do. I could be rejected, or even ejected, but somehow I knew the rebuke would not come today.

I silently approached to one side of where he sat, stopping only once, to view his still form. I saw his hand that hung limply over the arm of the chair. I stood lightly up on my haunches and, resting just the tip of one paw against the chair for support, as delicately as I had never done with Sara, I touched my nose on the tip of one of his fingers. In one, small, quick movement, his had flickered, as he looked down at me suddenly. For two short seconds, our eyes held. Then, sweet submission for us both, as he sighed lightly, not pulling back, but reaching slowly to the top of my head, as I welcomed his touch with a slow blink and purring. Still poised there, I relaxed slightly, as he scratched me between my ears. He watched his hand caressing my head, as if it was a foreign thing he did not understand, and by which he was fascinated. As easily as his welcome came, I jumped into his lap. He was still silent, as I hunched down and remained still, letting his hand find its easy way down the soft fur of my back. I nestled carefully, then curled my tail around to settle in, asking permission by small degrees. It was not for me that I asked, it was for him. I continued to purr, closing my eyes, remaining still, not demanding anything, only offering whatever unspoken comfort my presence gave.

As he continued to softly pet my back, I felt, rather than saw, him relax back further against the chair. He never spoke, but I could hear his tearful breathing, and felt the shake of the quiet sobs.

He never knew when I slipped out from under his slumbering hand and onto the floor. The moment had passed, and I stepped noiselessly out of the room, and on with my day. I found a spot on the floor where the sun came through a window, and sat down to lick the salty dampness from my fur.

~~~

James and I never did become bosom friends like Sara and me. However, I never entered that room with as great a trepidation as I had before. I even revisited that lap on many other occasions. Those scatting ejections from his chair still occurred, but my flight, from that time forward, was more drama than fright, and I found it amusing that James chose to keep our adjusted relationship something less than obvious.

Chapter Fourteen

I sat on a sun-warmed step in front of the house, serenely and methodically washing my paws and face. It was many months later, and our family routine had long returned. I had grown to full stature by now. I was a pampered companion, and a proud hunter. I was lazy on most days, and regressed to kitten play on other days.

Breakfast was delightful today. Sara had surprised me with one of my treats which she doled out to me occasionally. After satisfying myself that face and whiskers were clean, I sighed contentedly and looked around at the morning. I perked and twitched my ears at every sound and my cat eyes took in every movement keenly. Several birds caught my attention, as they fluttered here and there. I half-heartedly walked down the steps and in their general direction of activity. I got lazy again on the way, as the birds flew off from my approach. I sat down in the grass. A breeze came against my face and I breathed in the secret scents that only my cat's nose could decipher.

With no special plan for entertainment in mind, I stood and walked down the driveway, on to where it met the dirt road that curved by where we lived. After many such walks, it was a territory I knew well. I enjoyed the many sights and sounds, as I meandered in and around bushes, flowers and trees. I stopped to do a fresh claw-sharpening on a large maple tree that already bore my marks. The bark felt good, as I stretched my long body and spread my toes, scratching and clawing over and over in a fast motion. Sudden movement caused me to stop and look quickly into the grass beside the road.

I ran instinctively over to the spot to investigate. I saw the quick ripple of the grass again, and I knew then that I had found a favorite prey. Snake! I leaped onto the next flicker of it, as it slithered quickly to escape me. I made several leaps, chasing it, and when it cleared the grass, it came into full view, as it made its way into the open road. I hunched low, and padding my back feet back and forth, ears pinned back for more stealth, I readied for my grand attack. I was in mid-air when the horrible impact slammed me with a sudden burst of noise and pain. I flew out sideways, hitting the ground hard. I had no scream. I had no breath. I could not see. I lay, finally gasping, trying to find more air, unable to move.

When the sweet air at last filled my lungs again, I blinked and cried out. I tried to move, to get up and go home, but the slightest struggle shrouded my body with pain. In my daze, I saw movement over me. A hand I did not know touched me gently, and I could hear sounds of concern in the stranger's voice. I remember being gathered up painfully and being placed in something soft, and a door slamming. My world faded in and out, as I concentrated on just breathing. I had never known such pain as this, and had no other thought, except fear of the unknown things that were happening to me. Eventually, I came to rest on a table in the same place I was taken to get my shots. I found my voice, as the thing that helped me breathe was put over my face, and someone's hands moved over my body, checking every inch. I screamed for pain, I screamed for fear, I screamed because I did not understand. The voice above me was gentle, but not the voice I knew, and my heart and breath were frantic. Nothing I could do would give me back control, so I retreated into myself for the pure sake of survival. *Sara! Sara! WHERE ARE YOU? What has happened to me? Sara! What is that machine? What are they doing? Sara!* –

~~~

Somewhere inside the pain, I suddenly heard the voice I wanted to hear so much, and then I felt the hands whose touch I knew so well. Sara was here, and she was comforting me and crying through her softly spoken words. My dazed eyes finally found her, and I expressed my gratitude in my own soft chirps, and as she stroked my soiled fur, with her face so close now, I began to relax for the first time since my ordeal had begun. My sense of confusion and panic began to subside more and more, and, in spite of myself, I began to purr. Even the rumbling of it in my chest as I breathed in and out, seemed to calm me. I instinctively knew now that I would soon be away from this place. As Sara stroked my side, I heard them tell her how the car had hit me in a way that only my leg was broken, and the wind had been knocked out of me. No internal injuries, just bruising. 'It could have been so much worse by inches', they said. The driver was so good, they said, to bring me in quickly. All vitals 'were good', whatever vitals were. Well, if they thought there was anything 'good' in THIS experience, they didn't ask me.

As it was, my beloved Sara stayed by me, as I was repaired by the gentle strangers. In a short time, I was on my way back home, with Sara's sweet hand on me, the whole way. The ride was something I remembered, though I didn't enjoy it at all. The only pleasantness it owned at this point, was my Sara sitting close to me. I was wrapped in some sort of packaging around my whole girth, and I could not move my painful leg. Not that I wanted to, as even the slightest attempt brought on all my most plaintive meows again. I must admit, though, that these wails were useful for getting much-needed extra attention. I learned that fact well, and used it.

~~~

I couldn't have been pampered more than I was for the next few weeks. After I was back in my own domain, and finally away from the cold and unfamiliar stainless steel confines, I slept most of the time, as I healed. Stress and fright and pain, all together, were, indeed, very tiresome things.

I heard James say I had eight lives left. That was a curious thing to me. Whatever life I was on, in the count, I fully intended to make this one a very drawn-out affair. It was a confusing point, and I decided that humans tended to complicate things far too often. With that, I closed my eyes, giving a great sigh, and continued on with my nap.

Chapter Fifteen

It was happening again! My napping space on Sara's lap began shrinking, as her tummy began to grow larger. As I curled inside her arms that circled close around me, I heard her humming little tunes more often, as we rocked back and forth. Some of the tunes were new to me, but they all gave me a sense of peace with her as I dreamily offered my own purring drone to her songs. As I fell asleep, she would tell me all about the child she waited for, absently gliding her hand gently down my back. I knew all of her secret prayers that God would let everything be alright this time.

There came a day when I was forced to find a nestling space beside Sara, instead of on her lap. There was that special excitement throughout the house again, but this time, it did not dissolve into the melancholy days of before. This time, when my favorite lap reappeared, with Sara's return, my competition for the space came home with her. The tummy bulge, it seems, was the reason our household now held another member. A baby. It was a source of joy, excitement, and motherly duties for my Sara, but, to me, it was the stealer of attention that was formerly given to me! I did my best to sidle my way into, around, and upon almost everything Sara did with this new source of noise and chaos. Sara was constantly removing, displacing, or shooing me, as she performed her many baby tasks.

"Get off that, you silly cat!" she would say.

She was quite easy and light with me about it, so I used my curiosity to gain whatever attention I could get. It actually became a rather interesting and amusing way to fill my indoor time. I found the most interesting baby things to climb through, get into, walk over, lick, bat at, and sleep on! I found another interesting thing about babies – they had a taste for the same thing that was always dear to my heart –MILK! I sniffed its fragrant and tempting scent in the air constantly. It came from Sara, the baby, and, later, innumerable numbers of strange little things called baby bottles. They were a far cry from the little bowl from which I learned to drink milk, but much more fun when empty!

   I perfected the dive-and-ram attack on them, when they were all lined up, empty, in a row. Sara, anticipating my intentions, would run quickly to try and catch them from disaster, but she was never quick enough for my stealth and burst forth strategy. I think she thought it comical, as she often laughed as she shook her head and yelled my name, as the bottles went flying in all directions. I enjoyed it immensely, and learned quickly to recognize the sounds of her bottle washing. I would stop whatever occupation engaged me at the moment, and go running to my place of observance in the kitchen. There were times, however, that I was surprised to find James helping out with the bottle projects. At these times, I learned to postpone my empty bottle attacks to another day. James did not find my antics half so amusing as Sara did. I was quite willing to consider this and allow for a more flexible moment.

   There is something to be said for a lap stealer that smells like milk. Next to the little quiet, sleeping form was often where I chose to nap. At first, Sara removed me in no uncertain terms, but when she found I only sought a warm and cozy place to sleep, she eventually would only peek into the quiet room, and upon seeing us both quite safe and content as we slipped into our respective dreams, would softly close the door. My new napping companion was called Kayla, and as she grew in size, we shared many more things than a sleeping space. Sara managed to fit us both quite comfortably in her lap. We all three learned to play together, after some rather unpleasant encounters, as Kayla found how distinctly unacceptable it was to randomly clutch or pull any part of my body she wished. For some reason, my dramatic screeches only produced uncontrollable giggles from the little girl. Sara soon taught her the gentler ways of showing me affection, and less painful play. We all had many carefree days together. Kayla became a pleasant and playful companion to me in my happy home. My times with Kayla were somehow different, though, and Sara remained my favorite friend.

The curious experience of adding a new family member to our household happened yet again, as time moved on. His name was Peter. He was a lively, mischievous creature, and Sara and I both had to teach him a few things about how not to handle a cat. He was a typical boy, but we developed an understanding, which sometimes meant I just ran. Mostly, though, we did have fun playing together as the years went by. So, then, it was the five of us. It was my family. It was more than any cat could ask for. I certainly never asked for a puppy. I got one anyway.

Chapter Sixteen

As far as I can tell, there are very few reasons for the existence of the creature called a puppy. I know this, from personal experience. I had settled in to quite an agreeable routine with my family of caregivers. Kayla and Peter had grown to be almost as tall as Sara. James and Sara and the children came through the door one day, Peter holding a whining, wiggling, hairy SOMETHING in his arms. They had called my name, and I walked with instinctive care and trepidation into the kitchen. I remained hidden there, watching the door area where they now stood. All my senses were in full alert, as they finally saw me and came toward me with the strange little beast! I could feel my eyes become saucers, as Peter bent down, smiling, to put the unidentified offering up to my face. My keen sense of smell had already taken in its alien odor, and it had also, apparently, taken in mine, for we both, surprising each other, exploded at once! It bellered a loud yelp at me, escaping Peter's arms, and I had already gained a fast and lengthy exit in the opposite direction. I was air-born for a second, then the chase was on, and I was suddenly PREY in my own house! The family all came running in a group to capture my would-be attacker. I had the advantage of knowing the familiar territory. This little hairy assassin, however, did not let the unfamiliar slow it down. As my family hurried to catch it, I left a trail of falling objects behind me, as I finally found a place of hiding, beneath the couch. I resorted to a threatening low growl, as I caught my breath, and spat several times, daring the noisy black terror to come any closer. James finally retrieved the intruder, and after a very long while, Sara was able to pull me from my place beneath the couch, where I had implanted my claws into the carpet. I did not see the thing anywhere near me, but I added a few more hisses, and spits, just to reinforce my position. Sara calmed me down with her soothing tones, and assured me that the thing she called the 'new puppy', would not hurt me. Oh, really? Would she understand if I did not begin purring immediately, or step down quietly to go in search of the NEW PUPPY? A more gradual approach allowed the puppy and me to eventually meet. This took some time, but I had always been able to adjust quickly to the challenges of my surroundings. I soon found that I had a claw advantage over this mannerless creature. We soon had an understanding between us: He approached me when I allowed him to approach me, and we played when I was in the mood to play; I could eat from his dish when I wished, and he could never eat from mine, when I was eating. This arrangement made it possible for Buddy, which I learned to be his name, to join our family for good. Now, we were six. Buddy outgrew me in a short time, which worked well, as long as he held his respect. There were even affectionate times between us, and I must admit that when I curled against his big, warm, furry belly, I remembered another far-away time, when I had felt the same security and protection. As my purring would drop off with sleep, I remembered, too, that it was a very nice place to be.

Chapter Seventeen

I have a favorite place I like to go, to be by myself, where I can view everyone and everything below me. I have always had a desire to make my way up to the highest point possible, of any room. I have no idea why, but not knowing why, does not make it any less gratifying. It is an open place on a high shelf, with just enough space, between a vase and a bookend, to lie down. From here, I can look down and watch Sara go about her day, or James pass through on the way to somewhere else, or Kayla, or Peter, entertain themselves or their friends.

The only thing more enjoyable and relaxing, in the mind of a cat, is lurking underneath a chair or table, unnoticed, and watching people's feet go by. It is a form of stalking, although in a motionless sort of way. I don't understand a lot of what I see, but everything I see makes me wonder. I wonder why the speed at which people walk almost always tells the way they feel. I wonder why most of the feet I watch are in such a hurry when they go by. I certainly wonder why they have to put so many strange things on their feet.

Now, for a cat like me, you need only take a look at my tail to see exactly how I am feeling. Cats' emotions sort of run through us from our ears, pass through our eyes, and come out at the tips of our tails. I feel sorry for humans, because they don't have such a handy attachment as a tail, but I suppose their feet will have to do. Ah, the tale a tail tells! Straight up is friendly and curious. Straight back is neutral, but watchful. Curled around is content and settled. A twitch means nervousness, or anger, and, sometimes, pain. Buddy knows all about the twitch. A bushy tail means fright or fight.

We cats also know a thing or two about slowing down. While the people I watch seem to hurry often, and rest seldom, a cat like me knows the value of simply sitting still and contemplating the day. I enjoy this most, because it almost always leads to a nap, as it seems to be doing today.

Cat naps are truly often short, but highly over-rated. My highly-tuned senses often rob me of my rest, so there in nothing better than the long, deep sleep that is undisturbed, and no better way to come out of it, than Sara's fingertip trailing lightly along my nose.

Concerning the odd things people wear on their feet, I suppose I see nothing special about a human's foot that needs to be seen. I am quite proud of the sleek and silky features of my own colorful paws, and the exquisite curve of my tree-manicured claws. These are two reasons why I always take careful time to preen and bathe –just –so.

Enough for now, for I have suddenly become very. . sleepy. . .

Chapter Eighteen

There was no shortage of people, or places, to occupy my time. I was entertained in a different way by each member of my family, and I suited myself to whichever mood I was in, as to which one I approached. I had several ways of making my presence known. I would pad silently into the room and rub up against a leg, or arm, be it human or chair. I always started with my face, making sure the corner on my mouth slid against everything, leaving my scent and re-establishing my ownership. I would often trill or meow, until someone took notice of me. I would jump on or into whatever human project was in progress. This, I admit, was one of my favorites. Walking on papers, or open books, and knocking down toys, were easy ways to get attention. I was sometimes catapulted with impatience, too, but that really was not nearly as intimidating as they intended it to be, whether they knew it or not. I was adept at flying through the air and knew how to make it appear that I landed with dignity, on my feet. It would usually spur me to tear about, re-living my manic kitten days. They laughed at me when I would do this, circling at high speed, snagging things at random, as they scolded me half-heartedly.

I played when I felt like playing, and escaped when I needed to. I would spy buttons, or other little objects, on the strange things humans wear, and I would nip and pull at them. I sank my claws into anything soft, flexing and unflexing them. It was comforting, and reminded me of the times with my mother.

When I wanted to get down to some serious rough and tumble, Buddy was always ready to romp. He was a great deal larger then I, but gentle, and I held my own in our wrestling matches. He would dive and nip, pulling at my tail. I would screech in protest, ears laid back, sitting up on my haunches, whipping my tail, so that it thumped against the floor. Again and again, I would leap to the attack, onto Buddy's big furry form, and so on the play would go, until we both were worn out. We then would lie peacefully, side by side, Buddy panting, as I gave a great sigh, and licked all my tousled hairs back into place. Sometimes, I transferred my bathing skills to Buddy's big head. It was a futile task, so much area to cover, but he would let me do it, fidgeting all the while. When I finished, I simply walked away to find my napping spot. Buddy was left lying there, looking on, with the little wet cat licks sticking up all over his face and head. He was oblivious to how ridiculous it looked, and if Sara saw him, she would always get the giggles.

~~~

As time went on, and we both grew older and slower, Buddy and I put less effort into our play times, but we enjoyed them just the same. I never regretted that day Buddy dashed into our lives. There was a connection between us not shared by humans, nor could it ever be. Creatures like us, down here, close to earth, walk in a much different world than those above us. Our view of life is dense, active, and re-active. We both know the joys, and the stress, of living every day in this lower level of the world, in our constant state of hyper-sensitivity. It is alright, though, because it is the way we were designed and created, and it is the way we protect ourselves, it is the way we survive. In some ways, my senses always seem to be at a higher state of awareness than Buddy's, so I tend to be more nervous than he. In this realm of ours, I take in every detail of things that Buddy simply walks on by. Even as his big lumbering feet walk on, as he seeks out a place to flop down on the summer grass, I stop in mid-stride, like a statue, eyes keen, ears alert, nose testing the air. I hear every tweet, every squeak, every chatter. I see every flicker of a leaf, every tiny movement in the bush, every dart of a bird, every dip of the head of a flower in the breeze. I take it all in, with every careful step. I had decided long ago that dogs were good, and they did have their place, but I liked being a cat, for there was no other creature quite like me, and I would not trade that for anything.

Chapter Nineteen

I knew as soon as I awoke that something was strange. Buddy was very still against my back. I could not feel his rhythmic breathing, and the warmth was gone. I got up and slowly went to sniff at his big black nose. It was cold and dry to the touch of mine. I kissed his nose lightly with my tongue. There was a strange quiet and stillness that was not Buddy. His big wet tongue had always kissed me back. Something inside me suddenly grew uneasy, and I could not control the wail that welled up from my throat. I continued to walk around the room, and around Buddy's still form, wailing my discontent. Sara finally came into the room to see the reason for my cries. She looked down at Buddy, and saw what I had sensed. She knelt down beside him, and gently placed her hands on his soft fur.

"Buddy! Buddy boy!" she whispered.

I walked over to her and nudged her arm. Her hand went easily to my side, and she pulled me against her, as she began to weep.

I didn't see Buddy anymore, after that. I missed him terribly. I looked for him everywhere, called for him, for days. There was a certain gloom about the household, for a while. I slept more that usual, mostly because no one seemed to want to play.

Gradually, the house brightened again. Everyone seemed to fall back into normal, everyday life. I often stop and sniff at the place on the floor where Buddy used to sleep. I touch my nose there, gently. Sometimes, I sleep there, but not often. There is a draft, and my back gets cold.

Chapter Twenty

Evening was approaching, and I had no desire to stay inside. It was the time of the hunt. I often hunted on my casual morning walks outside, but there was a part of me that instinctively set me on the prowl at night. I would have an intense desire to hunt a prey I neither ate, nor kept. If I was inside at night, I would express to anyone who would listen, my insistence that I be let out the door. If knocking over various solid objects did not do the trick, I would offer my most plaintive meowing, in order to awaken someone for this purpose.

The door to the outside remained my favorite door in the house. It led to the places I loved the most. The garden, the grass, the little places that trickled water, the trees, the woods, the birds, the MICE! Now, birds were fun, and a challenge, but VERTICAL. They flew up and were gone. Snakes were few. However, mice, now they were gratifying and plentiful! Mice were HORIZONTAL creatures, and, after all, my sight was the most sensitive to movements in that direction. If the sudden sight of a mouse weren't exciting enough, the stalk and catch were immensely thrilling! My muscles were created to work in tune as one, so that I could be as still and stealthy, as I was quick and deadly.

After the kill, I carried my lifeless prey back to the house. I dropped it onto the steps in front of the door. I lay down next to it, proud and satisfied. I called to my family to come and see what

I had brought to them. It was usually Sara who heard me, and opening the door, she would smile, looking down at my offering.

"Oh!" she would say happily, "You brought me another present! Thank you! Yum, yum!"

I would rise, purring loudly, my head against her hand, as she reached to pick up the dead mouse by its tail. I never knew exactly when she ate them, or where. I can't say I ever saw her eat them. I only know she happily accepted them, and then they disappeared. This arrangement seemed to satisfy us both, and so it continued.

~~~

So, the hours, the days, the years, continued to pass by. I walked on in my feline world, here down low, always alert, watchful, observing, reacting, responding. I went on to experience many things; some with anxiety, most with contentment. I never again felt the trauma I had known from the terrible accident. I spent days on end with the family I loved, and who I felt loved me. It made growing old so much better.

Chapter Twenty-one

I woke from my chosen place on the soft carpet, where I had spent a restless night. James offered me breakfast, but I declined. I had no appetite today, only a need to be out, away from the family nucleus, away from noise, away from distractions of any kind.

So, I asked to go outside, and the door was readily opened for me. I walked out into the bright morning, moving in slow strides, for a few paces. I stopped to breathe the fresh breeze, as on countless other mornings. I could smell all the familiar scents in the soft wind, but none beckoned me to investigate them today. My curiosity, which normally triggered my morning rounds, was not in me today. Today was different. I began to walk, not knowing exactly where I headed, but sure somehow, that my destination would make itself known. I made my way slowly to the outer perimeter of the yard, stopping beneath a large tree, which was surrounded by small, tender bushes. There was a certain spot, below one of the bushes, which was grassy and soft, and there, I went down slowly onto my haunches to rest. I had intended to move on, but I stayed where I was. Before long, the desire to lie down overcame me. I was tired today. So tired.

I lay there, on my side, for some time, looking around, but not at any particular thing. As the hour passed, I dozed, off and on, then, laying my head completely down, closed my eyes. I have no idea how much time had passed, when I heard Sara's familiar voice in the distance. She was calling my name. I lifted my head to call back to her, but not much of a sound came out. Eventually, though, Sara's persistence served her in finding my hiding place.

"Here he is!" she cried.

Apparently, I had been the focus of the entire family, as, before a minute had passed, they were all around me, cooing and entreating. Sara soon hushed the others, and asked if James would take Kayla and Peter back to the house, while she tended to me.

It was quiet once again. Sara carefully nestled next to me then, there on the ground, lifting my head gently into one of her hands. With her other hand, she stroked my fur, ever so tenderly. At that, I opened my eyes to look up into hers. She was close to me, talking softly, speaking my name, and telling me urgently of her love. I opened my mouth to respond to her, as I always did, to let her know how I loved her, too, how I always did, ever since that first day she brought me home; how good it was to be cared for by her, how much it meant to me to know her lap was always mine to share. I tried, but no sound came, so I purred instead, for just a little while. She seemed to understand, so I relaxed and felt only the warm morning sun on my face and Sara's gentle hand beneath me, and I thought how lovely this felt, and that I had never been so content since the day I was born, when I nestled in the cozy darkness against my mother's belly.

The last thing I remember was the call of a bird, along with Sara's sweet, broken voice, then, the world as I knew it, faded away.

~~~

A man, a woman, and two children, stand sadly in front of a

small bush, under a large tree. There is a weathered marker that stands just to the left of a small spot of ground that is covered over with freshly-shoveled dirt. There, another small, carefully-made wooden marker bears these words:

Here lies POGO,
beloved feline friend for 17 years.

Amidst the sounds of quiet weeping, one figure speaks: "If he could talk, I think he would say he was happy to be with us."
I was.

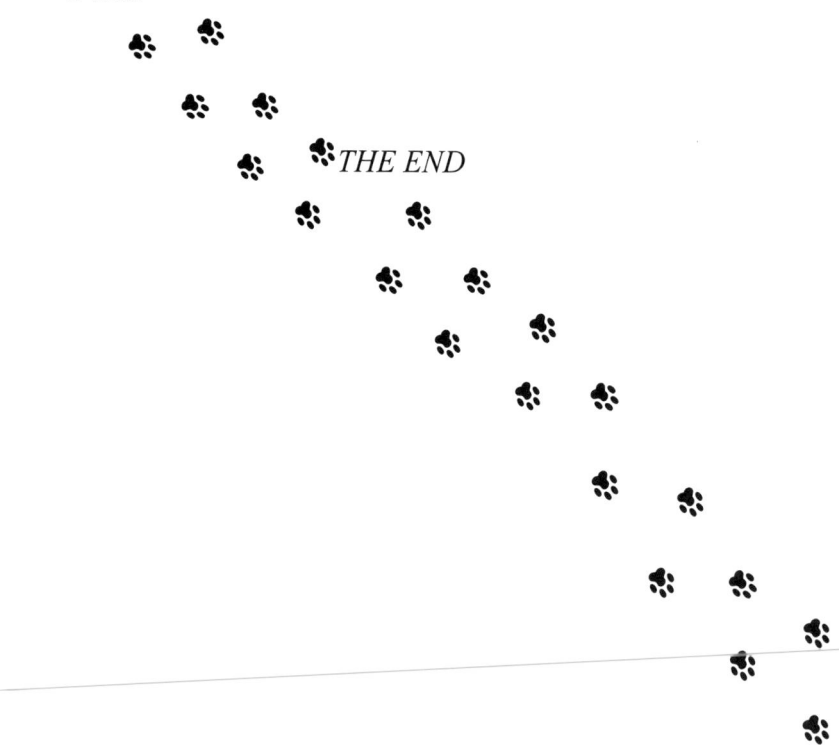

THE END

Epilogue

The Bible is open in the woman's lap. She softly trails her fingers down an old, silk ribbon, to its shredded tip, that dangles over the edge of the old book. A tear falls onto the open page, as she begins to read. A cold little wet nose gently touches the back of her hand. The little whiskers tickle her skin, and she is comforted by the tiny purring. A tiny paw suddenly bats at the shredded ribbon.

"Hey, little one!" she whispers, as she scoops the kitten up into her arms. She speaks tenderly, with her lips against the warm fur. "No, no, little girl! You will have your own!"

AUTOBIOGRAPHY OF A CAT

LAURA VIOLET NOVOTNY

AUTOBIOGRAPHY OF A CAT